Bingo's Big Adventure

by Julia King

D1001649

Bingo's Big Adventure
Text and Photos Copyright © February 2010, by Julia King.
All Rights Reserved.

Published by King Publishing, Morgan Hill, CA, USA.
www.bingoadventures.com.

First Edition. May 2010.

No part of this book may be used or reproduced in any manner
whatsoever without written permission except in brief quotations
embodied in critical articles and reviews.

Library of Congress Cataloging-in-Publication Data
King, Julia D.
Bingo's Big Adventure written by Julia D. King; photographs by Julia D. King, Morgan Hill, CA.- 1st ed.
Summary: Curous kitten explores his new world and meets animals that live on his farm.
Hard Cover ISBN 13: 978-0-615-34585-7
Soft Cover ISBN 13: 978-0-615-37032-3

1. Cats-Fiction
2. [Cats-Juvenile Fiction] I. King, Julia D. II. Title.

Printed in China.

For Ella and Wyatt, my little maniacs

. . . who love to chase cats.

And for Shmobie.
He is still missed.

Special Thanks to Karen, Bill, Mom, Holly, Jenny, and Suzanne
for their editorial review, comments, and technical support!

170686

Public Library

I am a new kitten to this strange place and my name is Bingo.

I have been locked inside the house for
an eternity since moving here. How I
have longed to breathe the fresh
country air, roll in the dirt, and
get mud on my paws!

Today the people let me out on the porch and I decided to taste
these dry plant leaves. The stringy fibers are rough on my tongue,
but joy, oh joy, I am happy to chew upon these wonderful leaves.
I am outside today and that is all that matters!

But wait! There is a world before me I have never seen until today.

Because I am a cat, I want to explore it! Let me pause and think about the situation. My instincts tell me I need an adventure.

I am Bingo, the Mighty Adventurer!

Open land is before me, no dogs. Hmm . . .

I think my life is going to be fun.

It's time for searching, it's time for investigating, and it's time for touching.

There is a large white object wearing big black circles in front of me. I think it's called a truck. Maybe I should give it a long, careful sniff to find out just who or what has been here before me.

I should also climb it. We cats love to climb, especially on those things we are not supposed to.
My dainty paws must feel it!

Should I leave my paw prints?

No! I think I should get down from here!

Hold on now! I see trouble.
It's big, it's orange, and it has
lots of teeth and claws.

I *knew* this place was too good to be true. Maybe I should run.
I could hide from this creature that approaches and hope it does
not see me.

No . . . It's too late.
I'll just sit here and see what it wants as it gets closer.

Look! See! It's Jimmy the cat.

He also lives with my new people.

He hunches his back, lifts his fur, and sulks toward me. His tail
is low. His face says caution. This must be his territory. Am I
even supposed to be here?

Will he be nice?

Or will he hurt me?

Cats don't always like to
be friends with each other,
but I really want him
to like me.

We *can* touch noses! This is going to be a friendly greeting!
Sniff-sniff, sniff-sniff . . . He smells like a good cat!

Hurray! He does *not* want to harm me!

Bingo the Mighty Adventurer
likes this new place. There are
new objects to explore and new
cats to meet!

I am a little kitty, but I am a big adventurer today. I see things
I need to do around here!

Now, I must look for bigger and better things to investigate.
I must keep moving! My body has energy and I want to feel my
muscles tighten beneath my skin. I want to feel the soft wind ruffle
my fur and the sunlight warm my back. I want to play hide and
seek in the dark shadows beneath the trees too . . .

But where can I go to find these things?

I know where to go!

Look at ME. I'm climbing a tree!

Since I'm Bingo, the Mighty Adventurer, I can use my body to scale this trunk like a squirrel. My arms wrap around the tree easily as I shimmy my way up to the top. I can scratch my claws deep into the chunky bark and it feels really good to my toes.

Do you see the big birds on the fence? I heard they are called chickens. I wonder if the chickens can climb trees like me . . .

The chickens move fast and have bright flashing feathers all over their bodies.

I want to chase one.

But I won't . . .

I can see that the chickens have pointy, sharp beaks. They are bigger than me, and I think they will probably peck me hard if I chased them.

Instead of making trouble with those birds, I am stepping higher and higher into the reaching branches of this tree.
Oh! The lofty view from up here is amazing!

What else is there to do,
    now that I have explored this tree?

        It's a trip back down
            to the ground for me.

Oh, no! There is someone peeking at me from behind the bushes.
He has a small beady eye and is wearing a bright red hat. He
moves quickly too.

He has been stalking and following me.

I believe he is a big, mean rooster. I see he watches over the lady
chickens *very closely*. He pays special attention to me! It must
be his job to protect them from danger.

Could I really be
dangerous to
a chicken?

I am still a little kitty,
so he should not worry.

Cock-a-doodle DO! I heard him warn me, "I am a Danish Leghorn Rooster. You can call me Mr. D. STAY AWAY from ME and MY HENS!

Since I am a cat, even though I am young, I know the chickens would probably taste good. And those feathers in my mouth would put me in a happy frenzy.

I observe that Mr. D has sharp claws called spurs on his legs. If he used them they could hurt.

Can he see me?

I don't want him to touch my fur with a spur!

While Mr. D steps high, I will lie low. I can crouch and peek and sneak after him. I am being naughty, but I can't help it. Mr. D told me *not* to do this.

So why can't I listen?

It's because I'm Bingo, The Mighty Adventurer!

If I keep this up, I might not last.
If he sees me, I am fleeing . . . fast!

Mr. D's feathers quake and shake warning me this is *not* the kind of adventure I need today.

But I can't stop following him.

The hackles on Mr. D's neck are raised. His orange and red feathers burst like a sunset.

So I must watch him!

Oh my! Now this looks like BIG trouble, since Mr. D is after me. I can't believe this rooster can leap and fly! *Why do I still try?*

Watch out for his spurs!

Running away from the rooster as fast as I can, I scamper back to the open ground covered with little rocks called gravel.

I see the Tall Lady. She is the human who adopted me. I am lucky these humans had room for one more animal on their farm.

"Hi Bingo! Did you have fun today?" the Tall Lady asks.

I meow, "Hey Mom, do you think I can come home now? I may be *Bingo, the Mighty Adventurer*, but I'm really tired."

I am definitely tuckered out with all this adventuring business. It is good to find my way back to the house. I think I want to stay here and live with the humans.

I like to be near them, especially after being talked to and chased by a rooster. I can admit that he scares me just a little.

Now it's time to snuggle my favorite blanket and get some sleep.

My eyes can no longer stay open. My lids are heavy like a big stone that sinks slowly into soft mud, and sleep is taking me to kitty dreams where frisky mice run everywhere just begging to be chased.

Today, I walked, I sniffed, I climbed, and I observed my new world. I'm Bingo, the Mighty Adventurer, so there is much for me to do here.

But now,
   it is time
      for a nap . . .

About Bingo

Bingo and Shmobie (in the dedication) were both adopted as teenage cats from Town Cats (www.towncats.org), a no-kill rescue shelter in Morgan Hill, California. Town Cats saves hundreds of cats every year from euthanization at county shelters.

Adopting an older cat instead of a kitten is a great way to bring a new feline into your home. Older cats often to not have the same "fluffy" appeal as kittens, but are so much easier to assimilate because they don't climb the curtains or otherwise tear apart your home.

When you are looking for a new feline friend to bring into your family, please consider adopting older kittens and cats who might otherwise be passed by in a shelter. They have so much to offer and need your help too!